Race Ahead with Reading

stinky!

By Ann Bryant

Illustrated by Andy Elkerton

W
FRANKLIN WATTS
LONDON • SYDNEY

Chapter One

"Bill Brady is a circus trainer, only with guinea pigs not lions!"

That's what everyone in my class says. But it's not true. I should know. I am Bill Brady.

This is how it started. One day at school, Jimmy Frape was boasting that he'd read a book with 100 pages in it.

Then Dan Potter said he was the greatest swimmer ever.

Next Ellen Carr went on and on about galloping on her pony.

Then they all looked at me... like they were waiting.

So quick as a flash I made up a story in my head about next door's guinea pig. (It's called Stinky, by the way.) And next thing, this came out of my mouth. "I'm training my guinea pig for the animal tricks competition."

Well, you should have seen Ellen Carr's eyebrows. They shot right up to her hairband.

6

7

"Bet there's no such thing," said Dan Potter, sounding like a big know-all.

I just shrugged and said, "Oh no?"

(That made me feel super cool.)

But only for a moment because Jimmy
Frape suddenly said, "Prove it!"

Then loads of people were crowding round,
all saying, "Prove it, Bill! Prove it!"

Chapter Two

I didn't make it up about Stinky. He really can do tricks. Well… one trick anyway. I've seen him from my bedroom window.

He jumps over yellow things like buttercups and dandelions.

On the way home from school I worked out a brilliant plan. First I had to borrow Stinky from Mrs Buss, his owner. So I went round to her house. This was our conversation.

ME: Can Stinky come out to play please?

MRS BUSS: (laughing her head off) But he's a guinea pig!

Then she looked at what I was holding and laughed even more.

MRS BUSS: Bricks! Is that what you two are going to play with?

ME: (still polite) Would you like me to clean him out?

MRS BUSS: Super! Thank you, Bill!

13

I cleaned out Stinky's cage double quick then began his training. First I fixed ten yellow bricks in a line and put them on the grass in front of him. "Right, jump over these, Stinky!"

He didn't move. So I did a few jumps over the bricks myself, to show him. It didn't work. He just turned his back.

"That's very rude!" I told him sternly.

"Squeak," he replied.

"You are hopeless!" I said.

"Squeak!" he replied.

Chapter Three

I went round to Mrs Buss's to train Stinky every day after school. By the fifth day he could climb up twenty yellow brick steps, walk along a yellow brick bridge and climb down the other side.

17

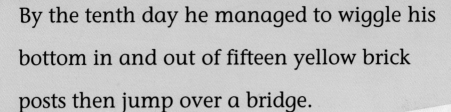

By the tenth day he managed to wiggle his bottom in and out of fifteen yellow brick posts then jump over a bridge.

"Fantastic!" cried Mrs Buss, clapping and clapping.

"Yes," I agreed, feeling over the moon.

"I think Mister Stinky is ready for school!"

First I had to ask Miss Tate, the teacher, if I was allowed to bring a guinea pig into class.

"He can do brilliant tricks," I informed her in front of the whole class.

"What fun!" cried Miss Tate, clasping her hands together.

I heard Dan sniggering, but I didn't mind. In fact I couldn't wait to see the look on his face when he saw what a great trainer I was.

Chapter Four

"Right everybody, nice and quiet please," said Miss Tate. We don't want to frighten... er, what's his name?"

"Tricky," I replied, because I didn't want anyone laughing at Stinky. I only wanted oohs and aahs and claps.

I set up the yellow brick steps and the
bridge and the posts. And I felt so excited
at that moment, I could have burst.

When everything was ready I took Stinky
out of his box and put him down beside
the bridge. "Off you go, Stin… I mean
Tricky."

But all he did was squeak
and sit on his bottom.
"Go on!" I said firmly.
But all he did was wriggle.
"Hurry up!" I said loudly.
But all he did was grunt.
"Get on with it, Stinky!"
I said crossly.

24

And he waddled off leaving a big pile of brown poo right in the middle of the classroom floor.

That made the whole class laugh, including Miss Tate. Me, I went as red as a dollop of tomato ketchup.

Chapter Five

Miss Tate called me up to the front

when it was nearly home time.

"You have been wearing that scowl

all afternoon, Bill," she said.

"I know. I'm cross," I replied.

"Maybe Tricky didn't feel like performing

today," she said.

"But no one believes that he really can do

it!" I said grumpily.

Miss Tate frowned. "Can he really, Bill?"

"Yes!"

"And are you entering him for the animal tricks competition you told Dan and the others about?" went on Miss Tate.

My face felt hot enough to cook a fried egg on. Miss Tate was going to tell me off now, for making things up.

"It's just that I was wondering," she went on, "if you could give me the details. You see, my friend has got a guinea pig. I'm sure she'd like to enter. He's very talented."

"What's his name?" I asked in a little voice.

"Stinky!" she replied.

Uh-oh, I thought.

But then I turned at the sound of gasps.

And this is what I saw.

Stinky had come out of his box and was balancing on his hind legs on the top of Dan Potter's yellow football.

I tell you, I've never heard so many oohs and aahs. It was brilliant.

And as everyone clapped and clapped, a big arc of yellow wee come spraying out of Stinky and on to the floor.

"How did you get him to do that?" asked
Jimmy Frape, his eyes all big and round.

Then Ellen cried, "Because Bill Brady is a circus
trainer, only with guinea pigs not lions!"
And I smiled to myself. This time it was true.

First published in 2013 by
Franklin Watts
338 Euston Road
London
NW1 3BH

Franklin Watts Australia
Level 17/207 Kent Street
Sydney
NSW 2000

Text © Ann Bryant 2013
Illustration © Andy Elkerton 2013

The rights of Ann Bryant to be
identified as the author and Andy Elkerton
as the illustrator of this Work have been
asserted in accordance with the Copyright,
Designs and Patents Act, 1988.

Series Editor: Melanie Palmer
Editor: Jackie Hamley
Series Advisor: Catherine Glavina
Series Designer: Peter Scoulding

A CIP catalogue record for this book is
available from the British Library.

ISBN 978 1 4451 2647 0 (hbk)
ISBN 978 1 4451 2653 1 (pbk)
ISBN 978 1 4451 2659 3 (ebook)
ISBN 978 1 4451 2665 4 (library ebook)

Printed in China

Franklin Watts is a division of Hachette
Children's Books, an Hachette UK company.
www.hachette.co.uk